Dancing Man

Thanks for Everything & Namasté 9/12/19

HERB TANNEN

PAGE PUBLISHING, INC.
New York, NY

First originally published by Page Publishing, Inc. 2019

ISBN 978-1-68456-768-3 (Paperback)
ISBN 978-1-68456-769-0 (Digital)

Printed in the United States of America

I want to dedicate this book to my beloved wife, Lynda Beattie Tannen. Also, to my son, Mitch; to my daughter-in-law, Jackie; and especially to my beautiful, wise, and funny granddaughter, Natalie.

Contents

Foreword

Herb Tannen has been wrestling his demons in pastel paintings ever since I've known him. That would be thirty-five years ago. Creating art from feelings of insecurity, loss, and heartbreak sustained him while he built his talent agency and became a well-known, respected commercial agent in Hollywood. He's painted, sculpted, and experimented with multimedia expressions of art, always coming from his deepest thoughts and feelings.

His paintings reveal the storm of emotions driving him to transform disappointments into achievements, metaphorically turning dark into light as he loved and lived. His relationship with Lynda, his beloved wife, led to a celebratory breakthrough of reflections in color. Her death took him back to the easel and to pastel painting with his fingers, reaching for other worlds to find acceptance and understanding. Friends and strangers collect Herb's paintings because they feel like mirrors of soul to be hung where they can be seen up close every day. My favorite painting is the *Dancing Man*, the painting for which this book is named. It's a never-ending reminder of the mystical dance that gets us through the night.

The entirety of Herb's book—writing and images—is a refreshing testimony to the transformational power of art to lift us out of any swamp of despondency and set us on our way, one more time.

Jane Alexander Stewart, PhD

Philosophical Fragments of Physical Possibility
By James Mann
Curator, Las Vegas Museum of Art

Herb Tannen is an elusive artist. That is, his pictures defy interpretation, and their evolution from one to another is so drastic as to dissolve all consistency and to challenge the viewer to find an objective coherence to this subjectively sprawling body of work. Yet such coherence is by now, in the new millennium, an old-fashioned value, a value appealing most to niche-marketing art dealers trying to show some consistency in an artist's product output from year to year. But it is not a value that must needs appeal to us helter-skelter seekers of new art with which to perplex ourselves. Looking to be perplexed? Look no further: Herb Tannen is here to confound and confuse your self-confidence as an interpretive consumer of contemporary art.

Two nineteenth-century literary men said it best. Walt Whitman said, "Do I contradict myself? Very well, I contradict myself." Ralph Waldo Emerson said, "A foolish consistency is the hobgoblin of little minds." Tannen's pictures are all improvisatory. He begins their creation with no plan or picture in mind. Image begets image, like procreators in the book of Genesis, and they all end up as one big dysfunctional family within the bounds of a single completed composition. Is Tannen's work Tinseltown Surrealism, venturing out of Hollywood to sin city for its first museum showing? No, showbiz values seem to have no place at all in his work. The work is sly, portentous, playful, positive, and a jumble sale of imagery coming to rest wherever it does like party balloons deposited by leaking too much helium.

The pictures may often seem light and airy, but this is very serious art. Each picture seems a new corner of creation in which the Earth has not four corners (count 'em, four) but dozens. From one work to another throughout Tannen's oeuvre, the styles just don't add up. The only thing sure is that each new picture will bring something no one, including the artist, can predict. Today, this multiplicity strikes this viewer as a great virtue, whereas in an earlier age, it might well have been seen as artistic multiple personality disorder. The diversity of the products of Tannen's creation should be considered the eruption of a constantly self-reconceiving imagination, from a deep well of originality renewed with each new sounding of its depths.

Tannen's pictures belong to a lineage beginning with the post-Cubist, proto-Surrealist work of Marc Chagall (1910–1914). The Cubist collage and the Dada photomontage of the 1910s and 1920s occupy the next position in this succession. Next in its intermittent course, one could place Surrealism's programmatic incongruity initiated in 1924. Some highly relevant work containing superimposed figural imagery by the lesser Surrealist French painter Francis Picabia (1879–1953) comes next, and then the mature work of the major American artist Larry Rivers (b. 1923). The late work of Salvador Dali, his so-called "composite" paintings, occupies the prominent next spot in the batting order. Improbably, newly discovered, obscure work done in Las Vegas in the 1960s by Katherine Gianaclis (1924–1999) completes this broken up line of descent.

Clear is the relationship of this lineage to a manifold type of visual composition being experimented with and extended by a generation of artists who are at the current innovative frontier in the visual arts and whose work the Las Vegas Art Museum enthusiastically exhibits. Herb Tannen belongs in an organic way to this movement, the work of which can be described in general terms. The movement's first principal quality is an original combination of imagery, from a disparate range of cultural sources, being employed in a single painting. This can mean imagery taken from the tradition of European art history, from the art of other world cultures past and present, and from more popular levels of art and life within the artist's surrounding and remembered cultural environment.

The second prime aspect of such painting derives somewhat from the first—a deliberate variety of styles, both abstract and figural, being employed within the bounds of a single work. The third salient quality is a nonunified picture plane. That is, various images and scenes in a single painting are montaged, so to speak, or overlaid; they are represented together, whether juxtaposed or superimposed one over another. The resulting work of art contains objectified subject matter, which, in mundane reality, could not occupy the same three-dimensional, earthly space or place.

Having said what Tannen's pictures have in common with this movement, one must recognize that his work is quite unique. Neosymbolistic Surrealism might be as good a descriptive label to assign it as one can find. Why is work of this type both appropriate and important at this particular juncture of cultural history? The following is a halfway thorough answer to this involved question.

Visual art was completely dismantled under two centuries of Romanticism, beginning around the year 1800. The dismantlement of technique and visual detail is not remarked at first, but it begins to be obvious in a painter like Turner, gathers considerable steam with Impressionism, accelerates rapidly through post-Impressionism, and explodes in Cubism and other branches of early Modernism when abstraction suppresses figuration. Surrealism then attacks representation from another angle (illogic), and this leads methodologically to Abstract Expressionism.

Since World War II, steadily, logically, and inexorably, the last stages of the process of dismantling both technique and content in painting have been carried out. By its simplifying, reductive nature, the further rigorous development to Postpainterly Abstraction and finally to Minimalism was a progress that removed all content and literally stripped art down, as far as technique is concerned, to its basic building blocks and physical raw materials. Now, it is up to artists like Herb Tannen to reconstitute the visual arts with cleared decks upon which to work.

How rich the possibilities for the reconstitution are is made clear by the wealth of imagery and styles present in Tannen's work included in this exhibition. Archetypal symbols float within fields of color and nonrecessive space. There are disparate, profuse aggregates of imagery on the one hand, and on the other, orphically austere, ritualistic, quasi-religious settings, with minimally few, portentous-looking physical properties, either noumenal or ominous in their serenity. Then there is the surprising phenomenon of Tannen's sculpture, nicely represented here. Carved from driftwood, with the same nonprescriptive, innocent aimlessness with which he begins his two-dimensional works, these pieces are fascinating in their unidentifiable forms; their formless, philosophical fragments of physical possibility, and their new birth or fractally infinite nature.

In their conception and concretion of beauty hitherto nonexistent, Tannen's sculptures leave us with the same gratitude his pictures do. We are happy to be enriched by these objects and mystery scenes, extending as they do our notion of what it's possible for the world to contain, meanings of depth we would have no access to, without Herb Tannen's particular, profuse, strange gift of creation.

I'm proud to have recognized your genius when I did!
—James Mann

Prologue

I am Herb Tannen, longtime Hollywood agent and artist. The first profession enabled me to pursue the second—art, my life's blood, and passion. When I was ten, I started making art as a means of escaping into another reality. Through the years, my childhood talent for drawing and painting evolved into a window through which I could reveal and understand my deepest emotions.

My creative process starts as I enter my studio, my sanctuary, a place to put aside all other thoughts but the making of a painting. The blank canvas is the door to an unknown adventure. As soon as I begin to form the first step and pick a color, I make a move with it on the canvas. With these acts, I begin the process. As the picture evolves, there comes an "aha" moment. It could come after a short period of time or an extended period depending on where, along the road, enough subject matter reveals a definite direction.

My process is as much meditation as creation. The decisions I make as I discover the essence of a picture are a mystery of the moment. They form shifts between the quietude of meditation and activity of creation. Decisions vary based on the colors I choose to bring a painting forward into expressions as well as shapes and any additional symbols that advance the narrative. I have worked like this with hundreds of paintings, coming away time and time again with my passion for life reaffirmed.

In the book ahead, I share with you the results of my process of painting that turn negatives in my thinking, beliefs, and life into positives. Using information I learned in therapy and the revelations my art reveals, I take the collection of emotions that zigzag in the middle of my ego and put them into the forefront of my mind. This comes without the distraction that the ego carries with it all the time.

My life is now exciting and fulfilling. I live in the present moment. I fill my life with art, music, family, friends, gardening, and a constant curiosity in life. With these things, I am never bored. I start each day with a mantra: "What adventures will be available to me, I must remain open." At eighty-six years old, my mind and creativity are still alive.

Namaste.

X
Pastel on mat board
45" × 32"
1994

Childhood

It is 1935, the depression years. I am three years old, and my earliest memories are of feeling insecure and alone. Fear of being punished has left me off-balance. Where did it come from, and what did I do to deserve this?

My family lived on Brighton Third Street in Brooklyn, New York. Our apartment was on the first floor. My crib was next to the window facing the street. We were a half-block from the Atlantic Ocean. There was my brother, Sheldon, two years older than me; my father, Charlie; and my mother, Pauline.

I had mixed feelings about living there. I remember it was the beginning of my nightmares, many of them linked, at the time, to a long, dark, crooked hallway that had three corners in it. In my dreams, in the middle of the night, I was trying to get down the hallway and out of the apartment. There was a boogieman hiding behind one of the corners waiting to get me. I tried, but there never seemed a way I could get past him. I feared he would punish me.

For reasons I did not understand at the time, early one morning during the summer, I decided to open and climb out of the bedroom window in my pajamas and walk to the beach before my mother arose. When my mother discovered I was missing, she became frantic. She could not understand my being missing. I don't remember if she called the police. Eventually, I was found wandering the beach and brought home. My mother asked me about being hungry. I said when that happened, I would walk over to people eating and ask for food. They always obliged. The next night, when I was going to bed, my mother decided to pin a note to my pajamas with my name, address, and phone number, requesting that whomever encountered me to notify my mother. I did climb out from the window again the next morning and was found by someone and returned home. I was punished by both my mother and father and did not do that again.

My father was born in the United States to German immigrant farmers. He was one of four. His parents were unaffectionate. My father had hated his own father. They were quiet, nonaffectionate, nonconversational, and strict. I did not enjoy being around them.

My mother was the oldest of four children whose family came from Russia in the early 1900s. They were immigrants and middle-class Orthodox Jews. While my mother's parents were very religious, my own family was not. In their belief system, my grandparents did not eat bacon, did not drive on Saturday, and abided by a number of other beliefs. My grandfather did well in business and helped my mother financially for many years. My father didn't make a decent salary, so having my grandfather's assistance helped us to largely avoid the stresses of the depression.

My mother worked in an office in her early twenties before she married and had children. My father tried different jobs but ended up as a salesman for a small, not very good brewery. He was always the life of the party at any event we attended. It occurred to me later on that he was like Willy Loman from *Death of a Salesman*, going from client to client telling jokes and making them laugh until they gave him a small order. My mother had a lovely face but was quiet and a bit introverted. My father, I'm sure, was a catch for her. She was often embarrassed at parties when my father would tell off-color jokes. Later on, people said my father married up in class.

I loved my mother's parents. They were warm, fun, and caring. My grandmother, Sophie, was a wonderful cook, and I always looked forward to the times she'd make blintzes, special doughnuts, chicken dishes, and matzo ball soup—typical Orthodox Jewish food. In contrast, my mother was a terrible cook with no sense of taste. I had to put ketchup on almost everything my mother made just to give it some flavor. Grandma Sophie and Grandpa Hyman always had smiles and a kind word. He and Sophie were always so generous with their affection. On special holidays, Hyman would dance around with a big smile on his face. Sophie would hug me often, something I dearly needed. It made me happy and gave me a feeling of security.

At the same time, I started to feel a lack of love from my mother. She rarely kissed or held me. I thought this was strange. My experiences from what I saw in movies, plus the way I saw other mothers acting toward their children, confused and saddened me. My mother seemed to favor my brother with her attention. She constantly complained that I was "difficult," which made me feel very sad. No matter how I tried, I could not win her approval. From that same early age, I started to have constant nightmares. Whatever I did seemed to always get me into trouble and make my mother angry. One time, my mother found out that I was climbing over the neighbors' backyard sheds and judged me harshly for it. In the following years, I felt an intense pressure to please my mother and to find some way to gain her approval.

What was happening? I was being punished both in my dreams and in waking life, by both my mother and my brother. Was I a bad child? My mother said so often. Why would she say that? What did I do to either of them? I just wanted to get away and hide.

As an adult, it eventually dawned on me that my nightmares and my mother's actions toward me were connected and that "escaping" out the front window must have been part of it as well.

I loved my dad. He hugged and kissed me often. He had a mustache that felt strange on my face, but I didn't mind because I needed and loved his affection. He would often have me sit on his lap.

He was a good swimmer and taught me how to swim. He decided that I should play a role in his joke telling and taught me a lot of the ones that he knew. When I reached about ten or so, he would tell me, at parties, to repeat jokes, which I did. People were impressed. Telling jokes became so embedded in my mind that years later, when I started dating, I would spend the evening telling my date jokes. Much to my chagrin, this behavior didn't encourage any extended relationships.

My father was also a very good dancer, so I decided to become one later on as well. I guess I wanted to be like my father because everybody liked him.

The good thing about living in Brighton Beach was swimming in the Atlantic Ocean in the summer. It made me feel free to be both floating and swimming in the ocean. I especially loved swimming underwater. Years later, I would test myself to see how long I could hold my breath. I managed to build up this ability to a little over two minutes.

I can remember my mother standing at the edge of the water and yelling at me not to go too far out. My reply was usually just to swim even further out into the ocean until I couldn't hear her anymore. That sense of power, to hold her attention, pleased me. When I came in from the surf later, my mother would again complain that I was constantly causing her aggravation.

Because we were so close to the beach, we could always beat the crowds to get a good spot on the sand. In the summer, thousands of people, wanting to escape the heat of the city, would come to the beaches, which ran for miles and miles. It was such a spectacle that the newspapers had pictures of this throng of people on their front pages every weekend.

I also felt lucky to be only a mile from Coney Island, which cost a nickel to reach by trolley. To the best of my knowledge, this was the first Disneyland-type park I was aware of. It had numerous sideshows—the Bearded Lady, the Lion Boy, the Strong Man—and other oddities. It had the Steeplechase Ride, which was famed for its height, curves, and speed, and the Wonder Wheel. There were always long lines waiting to get onto both rides. I thought Coney Island was magical.

And then there was the famous Nathan's, which drew people and visitors from all over the world to partake of their hot dogs, orange drinks, and other assorted goodies. I loved them. On the weekends, crowds of men and women, dressed to the nines, came down from New York City after attending shows on Broadway. They waited four or five people deep for these delicious flavors. Men in high hats got the food while women in gowns waited in the rear of the crowds for their share of the tastes.

From time to time, my dad would give my brother and me a quarter each and drive us to Coney Island. We could spend them on whatever we wanted, but it was suggested we save enough to take the trolley home. Often, we spent all the money on food and other playthings. When that happened, we would go under the boardwalk next to the park, looking for coins that might have been dropped through the cracks by men paying for stroller rentals. If we were lucky, we would take our findings back to Coney Island to continue our adventures. After that, we would walk the mile back home, which wasn't too hard. These were the only few times I could remember when my brother and I spent time together.

My brother often bullied and taunted me. One day, being fearful and frustrated, I picked up a roller skate and hit him in the head. I didn't really want to hurt him. I just wanted him to stop hitting me. He didn't touch me again until I was fourteen and we got into a fistfight. I got lucky and busted his lip. After that, he never came near me again.

I don't remember much about my first couple years of schooling in Brighton Beach. I only remember one friend, Arthur David, who I saw once in a while. Because I was socially backward, and because Arthur's parents and mine were friends, we'd spend time together at family events. We played together, and since I didn't have too much going for me with my brother, I relished my friendship with him. When we moved to another part of Brooklyn, I lost contact with him. He was one of the few people who liked me or who I thought liked me. Maybe that's part of why I blocked out those years in school.

When I was five, my brother and I were sent to a foster home for a year, without any explanation. I don't remember my parents visiting us during this period, nor do I remember much of that time at all, but I remember my feelings of isolation becoming even more pronounced.

I found out much later that my parents were having marital problems. It was strange, being sent to a foster program, as we had relatives like my grandparents that could've taken care of us. My parents never did explain what that was about. I suspect that, since they were stubborn, they tried to spite each other. In the end, my brother and I paid the price; and in my mind, it was punishment for being bad.

Another time, we were sent to a Catholic summer camp. At camp, the other kids knew my brother and I were Jewish, and the other kids would wait every day to beat the crap out of us. We stayed for a week, and I called my father every day to come pick us up. When he finally picked us up and I asked him why he'd sent us to that camp, he said that he wanted us to learn how to fight, to protect ourselves. All I learned was how to get the shit kicked out of us.

After we returned home, I continued with my schooling, but nobody in my family would help me with schoolwork. Left on my own, I was a C student, which prompted my parents to believe I was dumb.

Later on, my father tried to get me to hate my brother. My mother probably realized this and shifted her attention to compensate for this situation. My brother, knowing this, was always angry. He would smack me, or he would verbally abuse me. As much as I tried to figure out why my father disliked my brother, I could never find out why. He had gotten his side of the family to feeling that way by telling them awful stories about him. I felt it was wrong of my dad to ask this of me and told him so. Although I don't know the real reason my dad felt this way, he withdrew his affection from me. I felt I'd been abandoned by my entire family. I blamed myself and came to the final conclusion that I wasn't too bright, a lot of trouble, and unlovable.

Once, when I was about ten years old and we were living on Montauk Avenue, I remember doing something wrong and being told by my mother that when my father got home, he'd punish me. When he returned from work, I became filled with fear. I heard them talking and decided that I needed to escape his anger, so I raced out the front door toward my grandparents' house. I ran through the front gate and leaped up the stairs to their apartment, bursting into my grandmother's room. I jumped onto the bed with my grandmother just before my father (who'd been chasing me) came in to reprimand me. She threw her arm around me, shielding me from my father, and shooed him away. There was nothing more he could do, and he left. After a half hour or so of being comforted by Grandma Sophie, I went home and found that my father had cooled off and was eating dinner. Luckily, all I received from him was a verbal reprieve.

My nightmares became so intense during my teen years that I wasn't sure what was real anymore. I felt worthless, like I didn't fit into society. I thought that there must be a place for people like me. I had seen movies about asylums, and that thought crept into my mind. I thought that those people also didn't fit into society. The idea of not fitting in stayed with me for many years and created a strong leaning toward negative emotions.

Judgments of myself grew into an archetype of imagination that I began to call "the Judgor." More than a voice, perhaps because I am so visually oriented, the Judgor felt like an image. He began to show up in my drawings and paintings. He began to guide my life decisions, helping and harming with little interest in the outcome. He wanted control of me. My paintings became a window, through which I could escape but also get caught and return.

All this added up to feeling helpless and longing for someone or something to protect and guide me along. In this fearful, confused state of mind and ego, the Judgor, by my designation, assumed the role of master of my life and destiny. I was not, of course, conscious of this at the time.

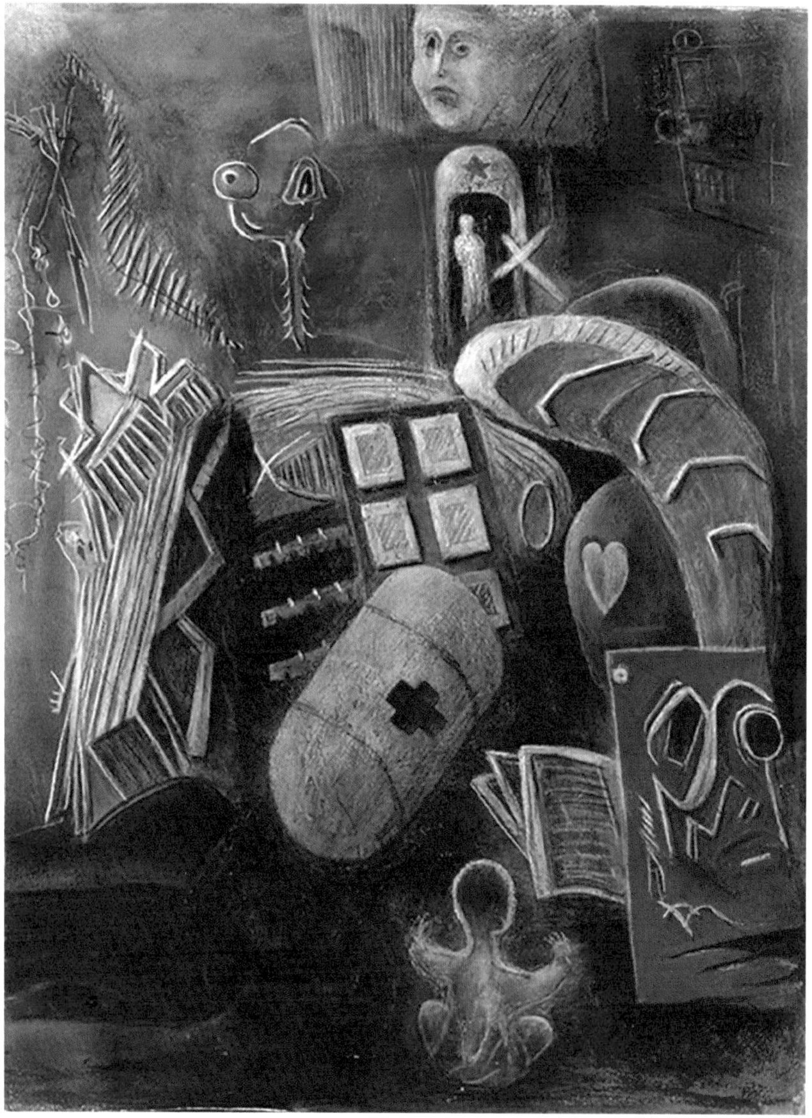

Night Dream
Pastel on mat board
18" × 24"
1994

Moving On

After Brighton Beach, we moved inland to Shepard Avenue, closer to my maternal grandparents. I remember how daring I was back then. The telephone poles in those days were always in the back of the buildings, spaced from one property line to the next. The wires hanging between poles were about twelve feet off the ground, and below them were picket fences roughly five or six feet in height. One day, I decided to climb a pole and, moving hand over hand, span the distance from one to the next. The distance was about sixty feet. Having total confidence in myself (at least while climbing), I went ahead with the stunt. It hadn't occurred to me that I might fall and land on the fence below, resulting in serious injury or death. But I didn't get hurt. I was proud of my daring feat and went on with my life. I didn't tell anyone about my adventure until much later in life. I guess I needed to prove myself, to myself, and that day I did.

We were only two blocks from PS 64, the school I would attend through twelfth grade. I made friends with a number of other boys my age at school, and we played a lot of street games together like ring-a-levio, stickball, stoopball, Johnny on the Pony, and three feet off. We also formed a social club called Club Varga, the name of which derived from a famous artist who created beautiful pictures of sexy women. We went as a group of seven to the beach together and acquired a group of girls who went to the same school.

I didn't date any of them. Years later, I was told by a couple of those girls that they thought I was stuck-up. I was very cute, and a couple of girls were attracted to me and wanted to spend time with me. But because I didn't have any confidence in my social situation, I put up a wall. What they concluded was that I was haughty and walked around with my nose in the air. It was a defense mechanism because I didn't know how to be with a girl. When I did spend time with a girl, I would spend all our time telling jokes instead of getting to know her, and they'd get bored and move on. Again, I felt that I was being rejected socially.

There was a schoolyard half a block from my house, so I eventually got into basketball. Because I was so short and not very good, it was hard for me to get into a game until my father got me a used ball of my own, which allowed me to at least get into the first game.

Still on my own with schoolwork, I did only fair. I was placed in a class for slow learners in my senior year. However, I did manage to pass most classes. My best memory had been creating a school song. There was a contest that I had won, but the school's music teacher went to the head of the school and convinced him to use his own song instead. I was very disappointed.

At about five foot one, I was one of the shortest kids in ninth grade. In another class was John Schwartz, who was much taller at about five seven. He had been born with only two fingers on each hand, the thumb and index finger.

For reasons I still don't understand, John decided to come after me regularly and often challenged me to fights on Friday afternoons after school. A lot of kids heard about it and gathered in the schoolyard, waiting for me to come out. I knew what was to come, but I showed up anyway. John proceeded to beat the crap out of me. I didn't tell my parents or my friends and just went on my way. The following week, the same thing happened. John challenged me to another fight and another. The results were the same.

During our third fight, John asked me why I kept coming back. I told him it would be worse if I ran away to hide and that I would be back to face him in school the following week. The fear of humiliation from running away clearly made the decision for me. He never picked on me again.

When I finished ninth grade, I asked my parents to enroll me in an art school. I had started to get into art when I was ten and loved the process and ability to create and escape into other realities. My parents told me that artists starve. I was subsequently enrolled at Franklin K. Lane High School on the border of Queens and Brooklyn. Strangely enough, it was backed against a cemetery, and the running joke among the kids was that if we flunked, we'd end up there.

Two things stood out during my high school career. I played, first, clarinet in the school orchestra, and I made the swim team. I won a 150-yard relay medley and came in second in the 50-yard freestyle and third in the 50-yard backstroke during my meets. This totaled seven points, which earned me a high school letter. I wore my jacket proudly. My parents didn't attend any meets or concerts. I also didn't graduate with my class, falling short in English, and had to attend summer school to get my diploma.

It is clear now that my poor opinion of myself was firmly in place by the time I graduated. I still lacked self-confidence in social situations. Because of this, I didn't have one date through my three years in high school. I felt isolated all the time, and my nightmares continued. My home life was no help at all.

Vulnerability
Pastel on mat board
40" × 32"
1994

Computer vs…
Pastel on paper
23" × 17 1/2"
1998

Reflections

Looking back at who I was and how I was dealing with life, I see that I had built an emotional wall around me. My fear was that if anyone got too close to me, they would see all those things about me that my mother had been saying for years. They too would reject me. With this personality and attitude, people thought I was just plain unfriendly. I didn't want to deal with more rejection. It was too painful and a reminder that these were major flaws I was stuck with. It became so embedded in my being that I did a picture, years later, of being in a darkened cave looking out at the world. It remains one of my most powerful creations.

While it was not a conscious decision, I made up my mind to not allow failure to interfere with my overwhelming need to prove my value to my mother and myself. I developed an engine of fear of failure that became my driving force for life. I recognized that I was persistent and was willing to put myself out there and take risks.

Nevertheless, in my emotional life, I played it safe. I turned off my feelings. Years later, I remember dearly wanting to change this part of my personality and actually asked God for help, even though I had never been religious. It took many years of therapy and life experiences to come out of my shell.

Year after year, I tried to prove to my mother that I wasn't a failure. But whenever I would bring up my success with her and why she might treat me that way, her answer was that it was intentional all the while and that it was reverse psychology.

When I was working at William Morris later in life, I would call my mother every year to tell her what raise or bonuses I got; and later when I had my own company, I would tell her how difficult it was but that we were making progress and how things were getting better and better. She was never impressed. I also used to send Christmas cards to friends, family, and business associates. I didn't like the store-bought cards, so I would write my own messages about where I was in life. Once, I wrote a very eloquent description and had sent my mother the card. She called me on the phone and told me that the card was lovely and that she went down the hall and knocked on the door of a college professor neighbor to show him the card. He asked what college I went to because I had written beautifully. She told him that I hadn't graduated on time with my class in high school and graduated a semester late. He said that for someone who hasn't been to college or university that I wrote very well. She called me back to tell the story and then accused me. She said, "Tell me the truth. Who wrote this card?" That was the kind of passive-aggressive acknowledgment I came to expect from her.

When I was fourteen or fifteen, I began to suffer numerous allergies and asthma. I was being treated by a doctor who was married to my aunt, Jinny. He wasn't a nice man and treated my father badly. When I realized this, even though my father wasn't emotionally present in my life, I refused to see the doctor anymore. When my mother pointed out that the appointments with other doctors weren't free, I said that I didn't care. I would rather go to a different doctor and pay for it from my Bar Mitzvah money. I never did go to another doctor, and later in life, I outgrew it all. I would follow through with this pattern of emotional honesty for the rest of my life.

Personality
Pastel on mat board
23" × 17 1/2"
1994

Working Life

For twenty-five years after my adolescence, my life was a roller coaster of experiences. From the time I was fourteen or fifteen years old, I held numerous jobs from working in a machine shop to being a traveling salesman. I mostly roamed the Midwest and was on the road forty or forty-five weeks per year. I was a Fuller Brush man and sold costume jewelry, storm windows and doors, chrome and aluminum giftware, pots and pans, women's dresses, and plastic table dressings. Because I didn't get along with people socially, it was very tedious. I spent a lot of time alone in bars, theaters, and motel rooms.

When I was around twenty, I returned from one such tour to a bar in Brooklyn. I was sitting with some friends, trying to figure out what I could pursue next. They reminded me about a time when I walked by the Arthur Murray Dance Studio and saw a sign—Teachers Wanted. They egged me on to apply for the job since I was a good dancer, but since I was short and shy, they thought I wouldn't. Of course, I got the job. After that, I worked for Fred Astaire Dance Studios for a time, and during the 1950s, I went to the Palladium where I learned Latin dances. I loved dancing and felt good about that.

Dancing was in the periphery of show business. I'd gotten a partner eventually and was working in Connecticut and the Catskills at dancing exhibitions. I'd met a guy in Chicago during my time as a salesman who was living in Chicago as an army reservist. He played basketball with me on weekends and told me that he worked for William Morris. He'd invited me to contact him back then, so I decided almost spontaneously that I wanted to be a theatrical agent. Selling talent was no different from selling the aforementioned goods. It's all a matter of communication.

When I was twenty-four, I asked him to set up a meeting with the head of the stockroom. At that time WM hired people out of high school and trained them over a period of years. The stockroom manager looked at me, in my one hundred-dollar suit, and told me I was overqualified based on my appearance, age, and habit of making more money than I'd get there. I asked for six months to prove myself, and he agreed to set up a meeting with HR. Stockroom kids made thirty-eight dollars per week. I told him that money wasn't the issue. I wanted him to know what I was about.

I got the job. We delivered mail, ran errands, and did all kinds of stuff. And somewhere along the line, if I lasted, I had to learn shorthand and typing.

Eventually, I became a secretary to one of the agents who worked in the nightclub department. Every city had nightclubs then, and William Morris was one of the top agencies hiring for entertainment positions. I worked there for three years at this point and was told that if I weren't promoted in the next couple of months, I would be let go. I'd also heard that the Chicago office was looking for an agent in the nightclub department, and nobody wanted the job because Los Angeles and New York were bigger markets. I called the office and explained my interest, and when he wasn't very encouraging, I told him I'd fly out and meet with him on my own dime. One weekend, I did exactly that and pitched him to give me three months. A week later, I was sent to the VP's office in New York, and he told me I'd been requested by the Chicago office to work as an agent. I got a raise, my transportation was paid for, and I wound up working there for five years. They just kept giving me raises and bonuses. I had accounts in Hot Springs, Arkansas, Minneapolis, Milwaukee, St. Louis, and others. William Morris had a great name and a great list, and I did well because of this and my persistence.

Around 1960, I booked Bob Newhart in Minneapolis and Winnipeg, and because he was already a budding star, I went with him to both shows. At a supper club in Winnipeg, I saw this really lovely, exotic woman who was working as a cashier, and I went to talk to her.

Seeing her triggered something in me. My first job after high school was in the mail room of the Revlon Company in New York City. The office was on Fifty-Sixth Street and Fifth Avenue, just down the block from the Plaza Hotel and the Fine Arts Movie Theater. They showed a lot of foreign films, which I saw on my lunch hour. I learned about many of the great European movie stars, especially the women. At the time, I knew very little about women and life, and so I was very impressed by the way European actresses were portrayed. They were nurturing, caring, passionate, and loving. This made a deep impression on my mind and ego.

At the supper club, I was reminded of these feelings when I saw this beautiful woman working at the club. At the time, I was twenty-nine, and my mother had called me recently to say that if I didn't marry that year, I would never be. The pressure she was putting on me, combined with the images and beliefs I carried from my youth, caused me to see my first wife as the perfect prospect that night. Thinking I could get my mother's approval, I married that Hungarian woman ten days later, despite the objections of friends and coworkers.

Three years later, we had a son, Mitchel. Chicago is in the pollen belt, and I was allergic to lots of what was floating around. So in the spring, I had to take lots of medications to ward off the symptoms, which in turn made me groggy. For my wife, Chicago winters messed with her joints and back. She told me she didn't want to live there anymore, and I agreed. I quit that job in Chicago and drove to Los Angeles in 1963.

At the time, I couldn't get a job in show business and turned to real estate to pay my bills. I did this for a year and finally did get a job with a theatrical agency. My wife and I divorced after four years of marriage. Eventually, I got custody of my son at the age of five.

Looking back over my career, I recognize that I did not have a lot of business training or college education. However, it was firmly in my basic MO not to fail. In almost every situation, I had the willingness to put myself and my reputation on the line regardless of the obstacles placed in my path.

When I started my career in show business, I was certain I would succeed regardless of how long it would take. I did well with William Morris in both New York and Chicago. When I decided to move west with my family, I did so, believing I had proved myself and would find a place for myself in the industry on the West Coast and rise to my personal best level of performance.

I started working for Abrams-Rubaloff at a lower starting salary than I'd received at the end of my career at William Morris. While I was disappointed, I put that aside and worked my hardest to do the best job I could. In five years, I was running the commercial department and had established a name for myself in the industry. When I realized that I'd run into a blockade regarding income and position, I decided to leave in 1968 and, with the encouragement of production company executives, started my own company with a secretary as my only employee. I worked six days a week, ten to twelve hours a day. Every successful booking was a validation of who I was and the progress of the agency. As my company did better, I took on additional help until I gathered a staff of fourteen. My company was considered among the best midrange agencies on the West Coast.

Three or four years after opening my agency, at an industry dinner, Noel Rubaloff came over to my table himself and told me that his agency had made a major mistake in letting me go. I was very pleased and felt validated. My success had only been made possible by my steadfast approach toward being the best agent for my clients. I was enthusiastic, passionate, and committed. I passed these standards on to the people I employed and built a wonderful, productive group of associates.

It was during this period with my own agency that I married my second wife. There was no love involved. I simply wanted to provide a family life for my son. She had her own son, and the boys bonded and wanted to live together. This marriage also lasted four years.

Finally, at the age of forty-five, I had enough of emotional disappointments even though my business life was going very well. I started therapy and, for the next sixteen years, dredged up everything I could to both educate and heal myself. In addition, I attended many workshops and retreats to augment my emotional education. All of this finally started to pay off. My thinking improved regarding emotional decisions, I had a better opinion of myself, and I became a happier person. My life was now more balanced between business success and emotional situations. I was in a better place to deal with the demands of life and business.

During all these years, I continued to create art, which I still used to satisfy my passion and as a balance to the demands of my company. My art helped me understand my problems in business and personal life and provided me with the strength of spirit and creativity to deal with them. Eventually, I started to sell my art. When I was sixty-five, I fell in love with my third wife, Lynda. It was a joyous union for thirteen years until she passed away from breast cancer.

During our time together, I had an art show at the Las Vegas Museum of Art and had been written up in magazines and newspapers. I also had a number of other successful shows at my studio. My wife was my partner and muse and helped me with all my work—even in business.

What I've Learned

The Judgor

From my appointment in childhood, the Judgor stands guard and is on alert at all times to protect and enforce a survival system rooted in emotional pain and fear. That part of my ego, nourished by nonobjectivity, holds the position of trusted ally and guardian of my emotions. He came into being to protect the child, fragile and innocent, in circumstances that were frightening, overwhelming, and beyond my control.

The Judgor has been endowed by me with all the necessary information about every emotional wound. He can color events with fear, which interferes with objectivity. He uses my acceptance of the information he has distorted to keep me from making changes. He is secured by my commitment to his schemes. He alone holds the activation key to a defensive system designed to keep the ego under his control. Every slight reinforces his power. He convinces me that I can't do without him pecking away at an endless array of raw nerve endings. Feeling doubly vulnerable, I am captive to his falsely reassuring presence.

Emotionally distracted and off-balance from the Judgor's insistent but flawed approach to problems, I reaffirm my lack of self-confidence. When you are emotionally blocked, and you live an interior life (the demon throwing you side to side), the Judgor is always present. Until I recognized that I'd empowered him with all the information about my fears, my self-doubts, I realized that I'd given him material to work with. Similar to your early life's injunctions, the Judgor starts to run this old movie—"you're a failure," "people are going to reject you," "you're not too bright," etc. I needed to step out of myself and use a way of looking back at myself from an external view to see my decision-making process.

I'd have to negotiate a deal with him: I'd acknowledge his presence but admit that I could do equal battle with him. Unless you're at a place in your life where you're willing to look at that piece of information intimately, knowing it intellectually does no good. It's whatever you bring to the table that makes you better and heals.

The Judgor had a good side, an ability to warn me of danger. It is up to me to discriminate between threats colored with fear and those within my adult power to combat with objective skills. In order to reduce the trigger-happy response of the Judgor, I needed to learn to recognize his abuses and begin to sort him out as just one asset.

The Judgor may hold a position of authority, but he does not preside over the final court of appeal. After sixteen years of therapy, I went up to Esalen in Big Sur, California, to undergo a five-day seminar on confronting my inner demons and do battle with the Judgor. For the first four days, the attendees dealt with many aspects of our own hang-ups in life. On the fifth day, we were to go into a room with two others to do a final battle. One person stood by and watched as the others—one equipped with a foam Bataca baton and the other equipped with a shield—did actual battle. I was in that room for two and a half hours, sweating, screaming, and doing everything I could to accomplish the task. Finally realizing I could not win outright, I decided to negotiate an agreement, acknowledging the demon's presence in my ego but also understanding that we were now on equal terms and that I would have the final word in any situation. This change of attitude improved the quality of my life and the ability to make better decisions.

Ancient Warrior
Pastel on mat board
40" × 32"
1996

Green Tree
Pastel on mat board
19" × 24"

The Power of Fear: The Major Tool of the Judgor

Fear colors and distorts the way I experience my life and decision-making. It can affect me subtly, lying hidden in the ego and rearing its head just enough to twist a perception. The influence is noticeable only as the top of the iceberg. At other times, it is like a raging dragon—frightening, bellowing, and throwing me from side to side with visions of dreaded consequences. It can immobilize me from objectivity and, as I retreat from a desired destination, fail to meet my needs and miss the opportunity to elevate my life to a happier level.

Fear cuts across the lines of every aspect of my daily existence, penetrating every level. It knows no boundaries, defies logic, and tosses truth aside. Fortunately, however, it also color-codes each personal wound hidden away. So in understanding the language of color and form, the fear that clamps down on a free spirit can be transposed and used as a tool for change.

When I can transpose fear, I step away from the major weapon of the Judgor. It draws me out of the safety of my childhood wounds into colors and fragments of images onto my canvas. This weakens its paralyzing grip.

Exposing the many demonic influences of the Judgor through the clues in painting and sculpture energizes and frees me. When I create, I challenge the Judgor, on my terms, to equal combat. I trade fear for truth. And though truth may not always feel good, I am empowered and am no longer immobilized or holding myself hostage. Then there are many more options to choose from at any given moment.

Fear
Pastel on mat board
18" × 24"

Thoughts on Boundaries

Boundaries give support, focus, and clarity. They educate, protect, and guide. They set goals, mark progress, and stimulate challenge.

On the other hand, they can intimidate, frighten, and imprison. The Judgor likes these. Fear, pain, confusion, and other people's agendas lead to distorted boundaries, which affect decision-making, alter directions, and cause me to lose my potential.

By recognizing the difference between boundaries that further guide progress and those that inhibit, I can illuminate my mind, settle my emotions, and once again take decision-making out of the hands of the Judgor.

In retrospect, my mother turning away from me when I was a child produced a precious gift. It caused me to expand my boundaries and turn to art for emotional survival. I escaped from the limitations set by my demons and found an extraordinary source of energy necessary to meet life's challenges in a seemingly unfriendly society. It also nourished my creative side.

I stepped over the line of shallow, external gratification to delve into the core of my being and embarked on a quest through my inner landscape. The results of these adventures show up in my personality as well as my paintings and prose.

My search for freedom from the Judgor's restrictions has proved to be an endless source of healing. Through all this process, I have come to appreciate and honor the nuances and connection of my mind, body, and spirit.

Boundaries
Pastel on mat board
40" × 32"
1995

Linkage

To this day, the vulnerable and wounded parts of my ego are attacked by the Judgor. When this happens, the Judgor draws from its emotional toolbox and brings up past events to turn them into even bigger aggressions. I become more fearful as it fills me with the same sadness and uncertainty that I experienced as a child.

This heightened effect interferes with my ability to reason, blocks objectivity, and distorts the present reality. While knowledge of the past is essential, when the unresolved emotions in my ego are mixed in, bad decisions occur.

At this moment, the Judgor whispers in my ear: "You didn't handle this right in the past, and you will fail again."

I know the ego is both enemy and ally, so recognizing where the dividing lines are becomes essential for choosing a more objective decision.

Understanding the mechanisms of the Judgor and the linkage between mind, ego, and heart is totally necessary to change the direction of my life. This avoids getting bogged down. I then gift myself with the opportunities of breaking out of the vicious cycle and moving on.

Linkage
Pastel on paper
20" × 24"

Night Vibrations
Pastel on mat board
32" × 45"

Creating a Painting

Creating a painting is like roaming around in a dark room. I am accompanied mainly by an intense presence of risk and compelling need to go beyond the safe and familiar into the unknown. There lie fragments of images and emotions that can both reveal and lead to the healing of old wounds.

At some point in the creative process, the room grows lighter, and the emerging fragments begin to reveal the essence of the painting. It then becomes my task to weave the pieces together, deleting some things and adding others, into a cohesive, artistic composition.

As I continue to seek out the core forces in my ego, painting keeps the door open to my inner world while grounding me in the outer.

I haven't always realized how this passion played such a central role in my walk along life's highway, but I was certainly a willing seductee of its mystical and healing powers.

Room of Hope
Pastel spray paint on mat board
40" × 32"
1997

A Tough Period

There was a period in my artistic life back when I did not sell many paintings. I sold maybe two or three each year instead of the eight or ten I was accustomed to. The country was going through a recession, and art was not selling well, but the Judgor peppered me with constant accusations that my art was not that good and my career was over. This filled me with depression and discouragement.

I struggled with this until one morning, I sat down and laid out my objectives. I recognized that the plan fell into three categories:

1. The creative process
2. The exposure
3. The sale of my work

Of most importance was my creative process, which was filled with passion, curiosity, and commitment. I had control over this.

The next was the exposure of my paintings. I had my garage converted into a studio with easels for private showings. I staged a number of successful shows, utilizing both my studio and the outside apron of the garage. I simply raised the garage door and opened my house, which was filled with art that I could show to a private list of friends and friends of friends. So I had control over this.

The final stage was the sale of my art. The Judgor seemed to have the upper hand here. I had no control over whether people liked or disliked my work and whether they would buy them. But focusing my attention on the first two objectives, I freed myself up. I am still delighted with this insight and brushed off the Judgor, who had been perched on my shoulder.

Options on the Road
Pastel on mat board
40" × 32"
1997

Painting as a Safe Zone: Staying in That State of Mind

The decision to remain in an oppressive, distorted state for the first half of my life was based on a number of pressures. I had given away my powers to another entity to protect me whenever the issue of change would present itself. When this occurred, fear, the major weapon of the Judgor, would be unleashed. It played havoc with my self-confidence, twisting reality and objectivity with reminders of past failures.

Then, the fear that once I would open myself and reveal the self-perceived ugliness inside me would result in the final disintegration of whatever was left of my self-regard.

Staying with familiarity under the guise of so-called safety (versus the frightening unknown) became the much lesser of two evils. Of course, the Judgor played a major role in this decision.

Recognizing this, I looked at my life and its direction. I came to the conclusion that I must take the risk of digging into my inner self and exposing those beliefs that had me headed in the wrong direction. While the process took a while, I embraced the adventure and finally regained control and changed from the low road to the high road.

I had enough objective insights that when shit happened, instead of falling back into bad habits, I was able to stop and ground myself and use this objective material to work through what the Judgor was trying to inflict upon me. At that point, I was making good decisions from an objective point of view. People go through life refusing to educate themselves, whether it's through therapy, meditation, or workshops, and stay in that same state of mind, feeling that they know what it's about and that the little voice in their head is going to be with them all the time, and choose not to do battle with the Judgor because he's going to beat the crap out of them emotionally anyway. The unknown is that if I go inside myself, I'm going to validate the terrible things that the Judgor is going to say about me. They stay with the familiar because they're willing to put up with the pain but not willing to do the work to step outside of themselves and see things from that point of view.

Thirty-Three or Not
Pastel on paper
23" × 17 1/2"
2000

Every Artist's Struggle

Every artist, when he has completed a piece, faces the daunting moment of confronting another blank page or canvas. When you create as I do, from emotion, it is especially hard. Past success offers no solace or confidence. It is at these moments when the Judgor becomes active.

He whispers in my ear: "It ain't gonna happen." "You've had your best days, and now you have nothing left." This adds to the pressure of not knowing where to go with the creative process.

But there is a positive side. As soon as I ignore the Judgor and pick up my pastel to place it on the canvas, the Judgor's power is negated, and I am free once again. I had overcome fear and regained my power over my own life.

My studio, because of this experience, has become my sanctuary. There, nothing but creation fills my mind.

In order to do battle with the Judgor, I needed to isolate and bring into light situations where, for me, he was active and at his most influential. I have listed some of those major moments when I recognize I am at my most vulnerable. This gives me the best opportunity to transpose encounters to my advantage and subsequent growth.

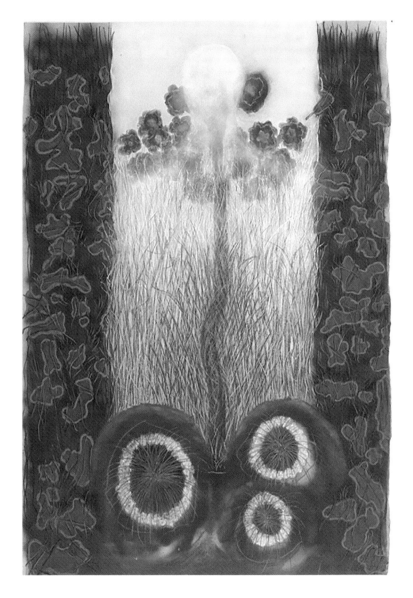

God in the Garden
Pastel on paper
76" × 47"
1997

The Judgor Is at Work When I...

- Use other people's judgment and opinions as a reflection or indicator of my worth as a person
- Feel small, helpless, and sorry for myself
- Dwell on painful memories and images from my childhood or later on as the source of my current problems
- Use my ego's collection of past negative images to ratchet up the level of a problem to validate a current distress
- Ignore dealing with present conflicts, putting them off, and believing the future will solve it
- Blame my personality flaws for my inability to face my current problems
- Abuse my body or mind, avoiding health and well-being for both the present and the future
- Allow distractions to deter me from dealing with the natural order of personal and career problems
- Ignore basic truth, which creates a conflict and stress between my heart, mind, and ego
- Am not listening to the other person
- Look initially for the negative in people
- Question my own intelligence
- Blame everyone around me for my problems

Bed Fellows
Pastel on mat board
40" × 32"
1995

Mantras

- I start each day with a mantra: There are treasures to be discovered today. I must remain open to receive them.
- Wondrous changes of life take place more easily and often when I am open and fluid.
- I remind myself that I have negotiated a contract with the Judgor that acknowledges our relationship. My affirmation puts him on notice that I will never acquiesce to his negative power. We may have a standoff, but my zest for life will not be immobilized.
- My body is a trusted ally. It will not lie and has my best interests at heart. I simply have to pay attention and recognize its language.
- Each step during the day must be revered. The destination of my journey will reveal itself.
- A commitment to honesty and integrity stirs an energy of inspired passion and directed action.
- Counting my blessings daily gets me on a positive note, out of my own way, and rebalances the scales of emotion.
- Passion puts me on the right course. When I accept it with respect and love, my thinking is elevated, and my goals are more desirable and attainable.
- At any moment in time, I know that I have the power to affect the direction of my life. It is simply a matter of making the choice.

Other Paintings Completed
1990s–Present

Mountains of Glory
Pastel on mat board
40" × 32"
1998

Ladder to Heaven
Pastel on paper
19" × 24"

Angels
Pastel on mat board
32" × 40"

Waves
Pastel on mat board
18" × 24"

Holy Man
Pastel on paper
18" × 24"

Subterranean
Pastel on paper
11" × 16"

Meditation
Pastel on paper
18" × 24"

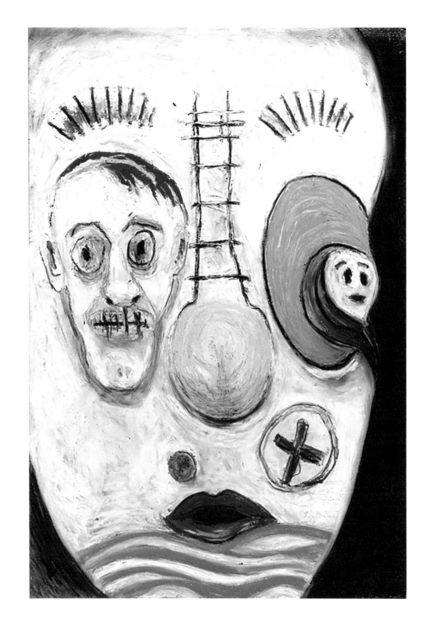

Clown
Oil pastel on paper
16" × 24"

Blue Coral
Pastel on paper
22" × 26"

Christ Ascending
Pastel on mat board
41" × 38 1/2"
1991

Plank
Pastel on paper
32" × 40"

Bird
Pastel on paper
18" × 24"

Triad
Pastel on paper
13" × 20"

Cave Dancers
Pastel on paper
24" × 18"

Blossoms for Rocky
Pastel on mat board
22" × 28"

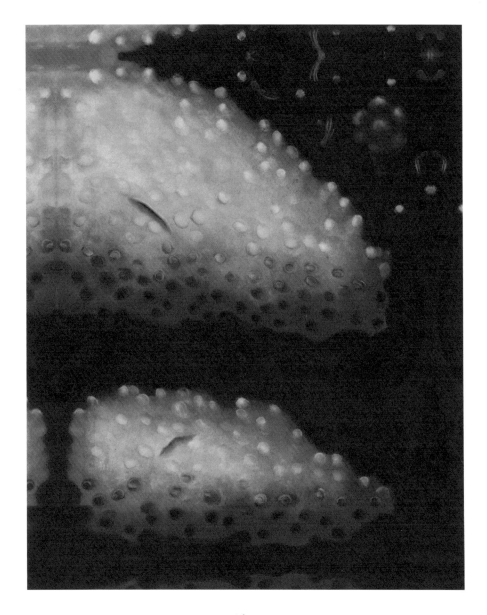

Alice
Pastel on paper
20" × 26"

City Energy
Pastel on paper
17" × 23"

Talking Heart
Pastel on paper
19" × 24"

Totem
Pastel on paper
18" × 24"

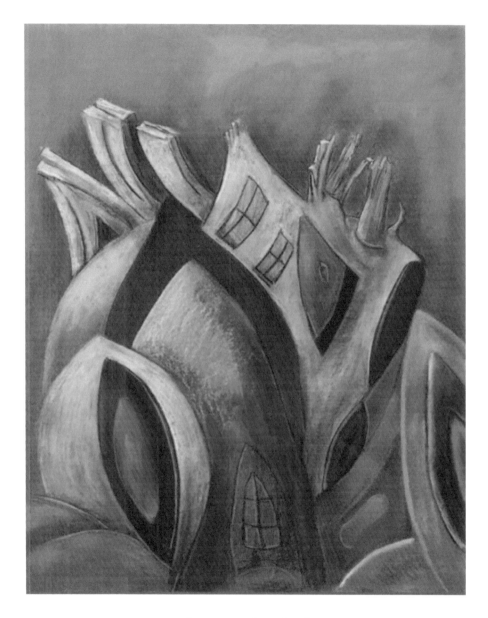

Ladies at Lunch on Sunday
Pastel on mat board
19" × 24"

Sailing Through the Universe
Pastel on mat board
32" × 40"

Earth Mother
Pastel on mat board
18" × 24"

Sculptures
1984–1988

Japanese Garden
10" × 28" × 10"

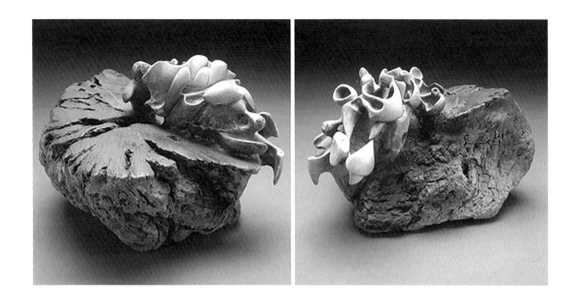

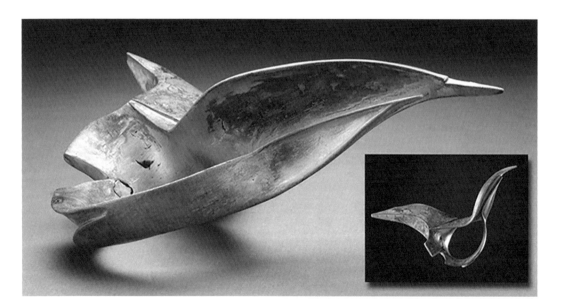

Upper: Anemone, 20" × 8" × 7"
Lower: Wings of Creativity, 8" × 14 1/4" × 5 1/2"

Centurion
11" × 4" × 5"

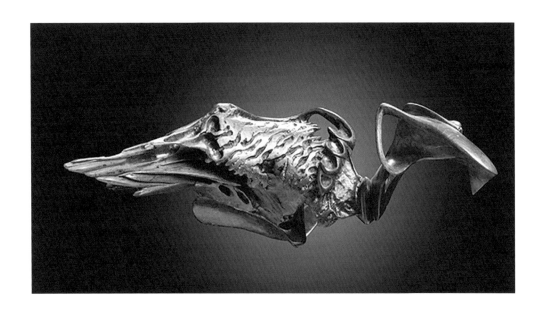

Upper: Mystic Eagle, 13" × 7" × 5"
Lower: Chalice, 26" × 7" × 4"

Man/Woman
14 1/2" × 15 1/2" × 8 3/4"

Androgynous
16" × 8" × 10"

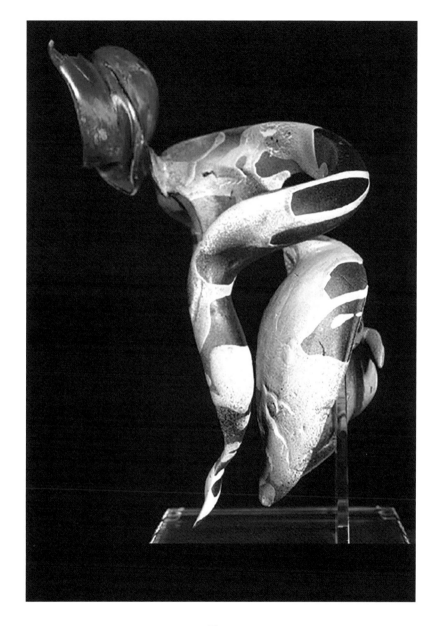

Alien
13" × 8" × 6"

JAS
14" × 6" × 7"

Wo/Man
13 1/2" × 7" × 5"

Desert Martyr
13" × 7" × 5"

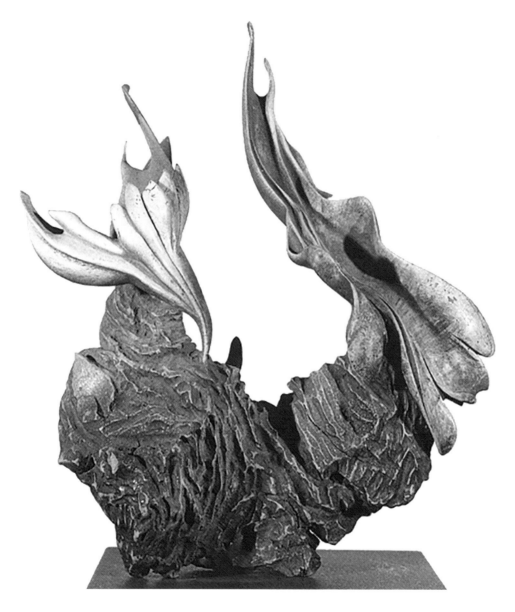

Passion and Grace
19" × 15 1/2" × 7 3/4"

Ship of Destiny
7 3/4" × 11" × 6 1/2"

Upward Motion
10 3/4" × 5" × 2 1/2"

Untitled Number 1
4"

Untitled Number 2
4"

Private Collections

- Dave Madden
- P. David Ebersole and Todd Hughes
- Roy and Rosalie Skaff
- Jane Alexander Stewart and Jerry Sicherman
- Lori and Albert Solano
- Denise Bankuti
- Katherine Radcliff
- Bryan Monroe
- Pat Benson and K. G. Scott
- Mr. and Mrs. Raynold Gideon
- John Font
- Russi Taylor and Wayne Allwine
- Michael and Nancy Dolan
- Herb and Sylvia Ellis
- Lomax Study
- Elna Lawrence
- Nick Salomone
- Victor Brandt
- Cleveland Clinic–Las Vegas
- Chrissy Orloff
- Marybeth Bonjour Geary
- Mitchel and Jackie Tannen
- Natalie Bergeson and David

- Boyd Willet
- Michael and Marilyn Stillman Clark
- Bev and Chuck Kelly
- Foster and Tanya Breashear
- Steve and Mary Riva
- Bonnie Pietila
- Rosanne Covy
- Cheri and Wayne Gregg
- Laura Beattie
- Bob Selzer
- Laurie O'Brien and Carl Weinberg
- Ron and Jean Finley

Acknowledgments

There have been two women who have played an especially major role in elevating the quality of my life: Lynda Beattie, my beloved wife, and Jane Alexander Stewart, who showed me the way to believe in myself, my intelligence, and my humanity. True Shields, for helping to assemble and edit this book; James Mann, my curator from the Las Vegas Art Museum, who selected me for a show that changed the direction of my art career; Denise Bankuti, fellow artist and friend, who constantly encouraged me; Bev Kelly, an old friend, who reignited and encouraged me to write this book; and finally, Michael Stillman Clark, longtime friend and artist who encouraged James Mann to look at my work.

So many more supported and encouraged me—Russi Taylor; Ron and Jean Finley; Lori and Al Solano; Mitch, Jackie, and Natalie Tannen; Foster and Tanya Breashear; Steve and Mary Riva; Roy and Rosalie Skaff; Boyd Willet; Jerry Sicherman; Marybeth Bonjour; Bonnie Pietila; Roseanne Covy; Cheri Gregg, and many others.

Testimonials

Every time I pass one of Herb Tannen's canvases, I take a peek into my subconscious—a mesmerizing dreamscape of things familiar yet just out of reach. Much like the films of David Lynch and David Cronenberg, you immediately accept what Herb has created, yet the effect is never predictable. Sometimes there is an instant connection, yet sometimes it hits you later when you are no longer looking. It haunts you. Sometimes you look right through his work, not even seeing what is in front of your eyes. It has gone straight to your psyche. His style is always pleasing, sometimes humorous, sometimes dark; and every now and then, there is a shock of hot pink that slaps you to your senses. I am very glad to own one of his most mysterious pieces, which my guests often think is new even though they have seen it many times.

—Todd Hughes

I've been to several Herb Tannen art shows, and each time, I have been inspired by his work and its evolution over the years. At each show, I have purchased one or two of his paintings I am most affected by. My staff shares my opinion, and we have moved our conference table into the room that displays most of his work—our "Herb Tannen Room" that is enjoyed by all! I treasure these pieces.

—Rosanne Covy

I have been a supporter and collector of Herb Tannen's art for several years. Herb's natural ability to work with mixed media in expressing his sense of design and humor has fascinated me. His broad range of aesthetic from surreal to almost representative renderings is impressive and, I believe, very collectable. I am a graduate of Otis Art Institute. As one who is well educated in art and art history, I believe Herb has truly touched the inner connectivity of all life. He has the ability to transform that knowledge into a work of fine art.

—Robert Selzer

I have been an avid collector of Herb Tannen's art for over ten years. I have five of his wonderful paintings. His diversification of subject matter fascinates me. One, in particular, is a portrait of a 1920s German era flapper that I call "Aunt Esther" and who I talk to every day. If I had more walls, I would have more Tannens.

—Russi Taylor

About the Author

Herb Tannen's theatrical career started in his early twenties when he worked as an instructor at Arthur Murray Dance Studios in New York. He then moved on to work in the nightclub department at William Morris Agency for a total of eight years beginning in 1955, first in New York and then in Chicago. After five years in the commercial department at Abrams-Rubaloff in Los Angeles, he started his own theatrical agency in 1968, specializing in voice-over talent. His sole remaining client is Russi Taylor, the voice of Minnie Mouse, whom he has represented for thirty-seven years. Tannen has been married three times. He is a widower. He has a son, Mitch, and a ten-year-old granddaughter named Natalie. He currently resides in Malibu, California, where he has lived for almost forty years.

CPSIA information can be obtained at www.ICGtesting.com
Printed in the USA
BVIW121904190719
553878BV00001BA/2

* 9 7 8 1 6 8 4 5 6 7 6 8 3 *